Susanna's bananas

Lesley Sims

Illustrated by David Semple

"Susanna!" coos Toucan.
"Have you heard the news?

RAINFOREST TIMES

SLOTH FALLS FROM TREE

Sloth fell from his tree,
when having a snooze."

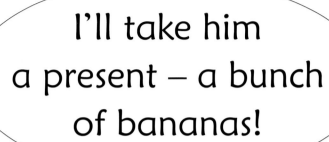

"And bake him a cake
full of figs and sultanas."

"How kind," mumbles Sloth,
as he slumps and looks sad.

"I feel poorly and sore
and my bumped head is bad."

And she juggles bananas,
the cake and a cup.

Sloth moans and he groans.

Try something else. Quick!

"I know," cries Susanna.
"A magical trick."

"Bananas!" says Frog,
grabbing one,
with a grin.

GET WELL S

She gobbles it up and then
throws down the skin.

Sloth still isn't happy.
He's ill and feels blue.

Susanna says, "I'll dance a jig –
just for you."

Susanna is singing and dancing about.

She spins round and round...

But Susanna can't hear.
She slips on the skin
and trips over.

OH DEAR!

Susanna goes
flying and lands
on her tail.

She stands, feeling foolish,
as Sloth starts to wail...

GET WELL SOON!

He is crying... with laughter.

"That did make me smile."

"Oh do it again.
You go flying with style."

"You want that again?"
asks dizzy Susanna.

GET WELL SOON!

"I'll help you," cries Frog.
"Just pass a banana!"

About phonics

Phonics is a method of teaching reading which is used extensively in today's schools. At its heart is an emphasis on identifying the *sounds* of letters, or combinations of letters, that are then put together to make words. These sounds are known as phonemes.

Starting to read
Learning to read is an important milestone for any child. The process can begin well before children start to learn letters and put them together to read words. The sooner children can discover books and enjoy stories and language, the better they will be prepared for reading themselves, first with the help of an adult and then independently.

You can find out more about phonics on the Usborne Very First Reading website, **www.veryfirstreading.com**. Click on the **Parents** tab at the top of the page, then scroll down and click on **About synthetic phonics**.

Phonemic awareness

An important early stage in pre-reading and early reading is developing phonemic awareness: that is, listening out for the sounds within words. Rhymes, rhyming stories and alliteration are excellent ways of encouraging phonemic awareness.

In this story, your child will soon identify the *a* sound, as in **Susanna** and **banana**. Look out, too, for rhymes such as **grin** – **skin** and **quick** – **trick**.

Hearing your child read

If your child is reading a story to you, don't rush to correct mistakes, but be ready to prompt or guide if he or she is struggling. Above all, do give plenty of praise and encouragement.

Edited by Jenny Tyler
Designed by Sam Whibley

Reading consultants: Alison Kelly and Anne Washtell

First published in 2020 by Usborne Publishing Ltd., Usborne House, 83-85 Saffron Hill,
London EC1N 8RT, England. Usborne.com Copyright © 2020 Usborne Publishing Ltd.